Topsy + Tim

go swimming

Jean and Gareth Adamson

Blackie

Copyright © 1988 Jean and Gareth Adamson
First published 1988 by Blackie and Son Ltd.
Reprinted 1988

British Library Cataloguing in Publication Data
Adamson, Jean
Topsy and Tim go swimming
I. Title   II. Adamson, Gareth
823'.914[J]

ISBN 0-216-92461-8
ISBN 0-216-92460-X Pbk

Blackie and Son Limited
7 Leicester Place
London WC2H 7BP

Printed in Portugal

Topsy and Tim were learning to swim.
Mummy took them to the swimming pool
nearly every day.

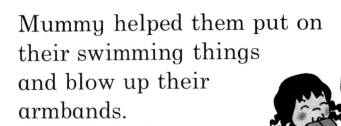

Mummy helped them put on
their swimming things
and blow up their
armbands.

She put their
clothes safely
in a locker.

They all had to walk through a footbath on their way to the pool, to make sure their feet were clean.

There was a small pool for beginners
like Topsy and Tim. It was full of
happy, noisy children.
'Race you to the water!' shouted
Topsy.

Topsy's feet skidded. Mr Pollack
the swimming instructor rushed
to save her.
'Never run near the pool,' he said.
'The floor is wet and slippery
and it's very hard if you fall and
bang your head.'

Topsy and Tim went down the steps
into the pool. Mummy went in with
them. The water came up to Topsy and
Tim's middles.

They held on to the rail and kicked
as hard as they could. Mummy did get
splashed.
'Keep your legs straight,' she said.

'Now let me see you swim dog-paddle,'
said Mummy. Topsy paddled like a puppy.
Her armbands helped her to float.

Tim paddled hard. He splashed more than
Topsy, but his legs kept sinking.

'Do you think you could swim without
your armbands?' asked Mummy.
'Of course,' shouted Tim. 'I'm a
champion swimmer.'

First Topsy stood in the water
a few steps from the side. Then
she pushed forward in the water
and dog-paddled to the hand rail.
'Well done Topsy,' said Mummy.
'You can really swim now.'

Then it was Tim's turn. He tried
hard . . . but his feet would not
float.
'Never mind,' said Mummy. 'You
must put your armbands back on.'

'Can I help?' said a kind voice.
It was Mr Pollack the swimming
instructor. He told Tim to bob
right down until the water was
up to his chin.
'Now walk along and pull the water
back with your hands,' he said.

Tim paddled hard with his hands,
then he kicked up and down with his legs.
'Look at me,' he gasped. 'I'm swimming!'
And he really was.

Mummy helped them to get dressed
and dry their hair.
'Won't Dad be surprised when we
tell him we can swim
without our armbands,' said Tim.

Dad was waiting for them
in the snack bar.
'Dad, we can swim!' cried Topsy.
Dad *was* pleased. He pointed to
a poster on the wall.
'There's going to be a swimming
competition,' he said. 'You can
swim in the beginners' race, Topsy
and Tim.'

The next week Dad and Mummy
and Topsy and Tim went to the
big pool for the swimming competition.
There were short races.
There were long races.

There was a race for children swimming on their backs. Last of all there was the beginners' race in the beginners' pool.

Mr Pollack blew his whistle to start
the race. Topsy swam dog-paddle
as fast as she could.
Tim was left behind—but he knew
what to do.

He bobbed right down in the water
until it reached his chin,
then he paddled hard with his hands
and feet. Everyone cheered as
the children swam slowly across the pool.

Topsy and Tim didn't win the race,
but everyone got a Beginners' Badge
because they had all reached the other
side.